W9-BNQ-293

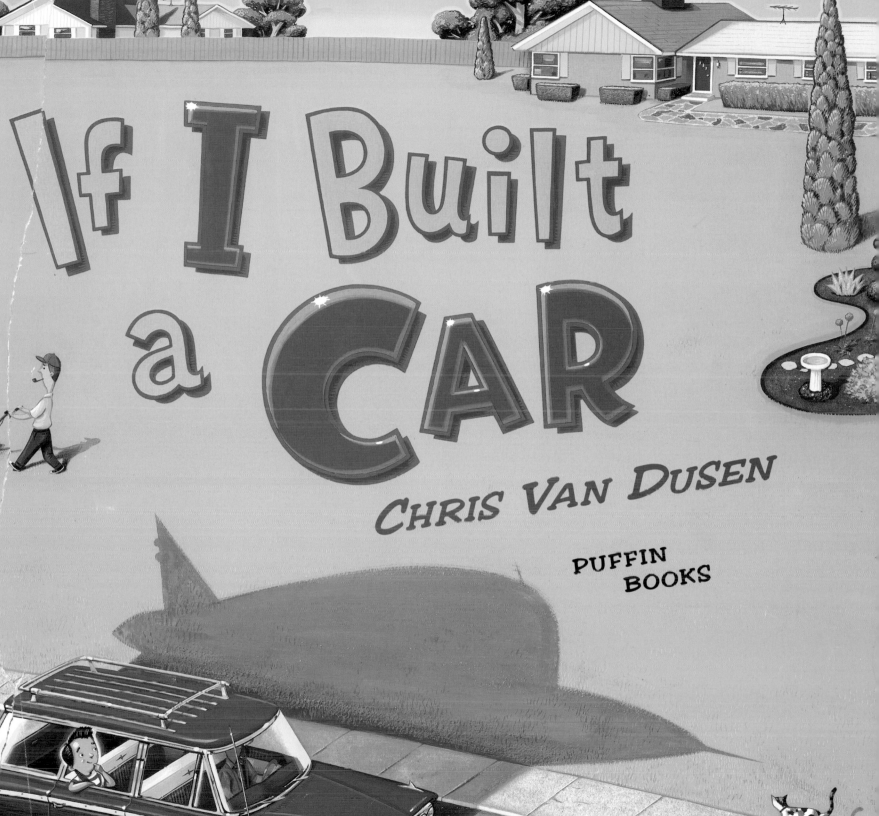

If I Built a CAR

CHRIS VAN DUSEN

PUFFIN BOOKS

PUFFIN BOOKS

Published by the Penguin Group

Penguin Young Readers Group, 345 Hudson Street, New York, New York 10014, U.S.A.

Penguin Group (Canada), 90 Eglinton Avenue East, Suite 700, Toronto, Ontario, Canada M4P 2Y3

(a division of Pearson Penguin Canada Inc.)

Penguin Books Ltd, 80 Strand, London WC2R 0RL, England

Penguin Ireland, 25 St Stephen's Green, Dublin 2, Ireland

(a division of Penguin Books Ltd)

Penguin Group (Australia), 250 Camberwell Road, Camberwell, Victoria 3124, Australia

(a division of Pearson Australia Group Pty Ltd)

Penguin Books India Pvt Ltd, 11 Community Centre, Panchsheel Park, New Delhi - 110 017, India

Penguin Group (NZ), Cnr Airborne and Rosedale Roads, Albany, Auckland 1310, New Zealand

(a division of Pearson New Zealand Ltd)

Penguin Books (South Africa) (Pty) Ltd, 24 Sturdee Avenue, Rosebank, Johannesburg 2196, South Africa

Registered Offices: Penguin Books Ltd, 80 Strand, London WC2R 0RL, England

First published in the United States of America by Dutton Children's Books,
a division of Penguin Young Readers Group, 2005
Published by Puffin Books, a division of Penguin Young Readers Group, 2007

20 19

THE LIBRARY OF CONGRESS HAS CATALOGED THE DUTTON CHILDREN'S BOOKS EDITION AS FOLLOWS:
Van Dusen, Chris.
If I built a car / Chris Van Dusen.—1st ed.
p. cm.
Summary: Jack describes the kind of car he would build—one with amazing accessories and
with the capability of traveling on land, in the air, and on and under the sea.
ISBN 0-525-47400-5 (hc)
[1. Automobiles—Fiction. 2. Stories in rhyme.] I. Title.
PZ8.3.V335If 2005 [E]—dc22 2004021470

Puffin Books ISBN 978-0-14-240825-4

Endpaper lettering by Tucker Van Dusen

Wienermobile™ is a trademark of the Oscar Mayer division of Kraft Foods of North America.

Manufactured in China

This book is dedicated to my mom and dad, who

* jump-started my curiosity
* fueled my creativity and
* changed my crayons every 3,000 miles

Jack, from the backseat, said to his dad,

This car is OK. This car is not bad.

But it's just a car. Nothing great. Nothing grand.

It's nothing at **all** like the car **I** have planned.

I'll work through the night to create a design—
Constantly analyze, tweak, and refine.
I'll study jet rockets and look at old planes,
Contemplate buses and zeppelins and trains.
To make it as smooth and as sleek as an eel,
I'll borrow ideas from the Wienermobile!

So sit back, relax, stay right where you are.
It's time to reveal my spectacular car!

You'll see that I've added a lot of neat things:
Flush fender skirts and retractable wings,
Three headlights up front, four taillights in back,
Plus two giant fins like our old Cadillac!
My brand-new design will be curvy and round,
With special jet engines that don't make a sound.
I'll paint it bright colors with accents of chrome
And top it all off with a Plexiglas dome.

I'll build a safe car, just as safe as I can,

'Cause safety is job number-one in my plan.

It may look like steel—from afar you can't tell,

But it's actually made of a polymer gel—

A space-age concoction that I just invented

So in a collision my car won't get dented.

It simply absorbs what we happen to hit,

And folks would be fine in the seats where they sit.

Come with me now and I'll show you inside.

I've put in a couch. It's comfy and wide.

Plus a fireplace, fish tank, and here's something cool—

The floor can slide open, and look—there's a pool!

Now step right this way to the back of the car
And note the red button marked INSTANT SNACK BAR.
Say you were hungry and wanted a treat:
Just press it, and instantly good things to eat
Appear in a flash! Anything that you please,
From hazelnut pudding to aerosol cheese!

After you've eaten you might like a nap,

And Robert the Robot makes napping a snap!

I've built him right into the back of the chair.

He's out of the way. You won't know that he's there.

But when you get sleepy and rise from your seat,

The chair spins around without missing a beat.

Robert the Robot will take the controls . . .

And he's guaranteed not to hit telephone poles.

I see you're impressed with all that's inside,

So start up the motor. Let's go for a ride.

A car that smells GOOD? Now that's something new.

But if I built a car, that's just what I'd do.

Inside the engine I'll add a machine

To capture the odor of burnt gasoline

And change it to something more pleasing to noses—

Like blueberry muffins or freshly picked roses.

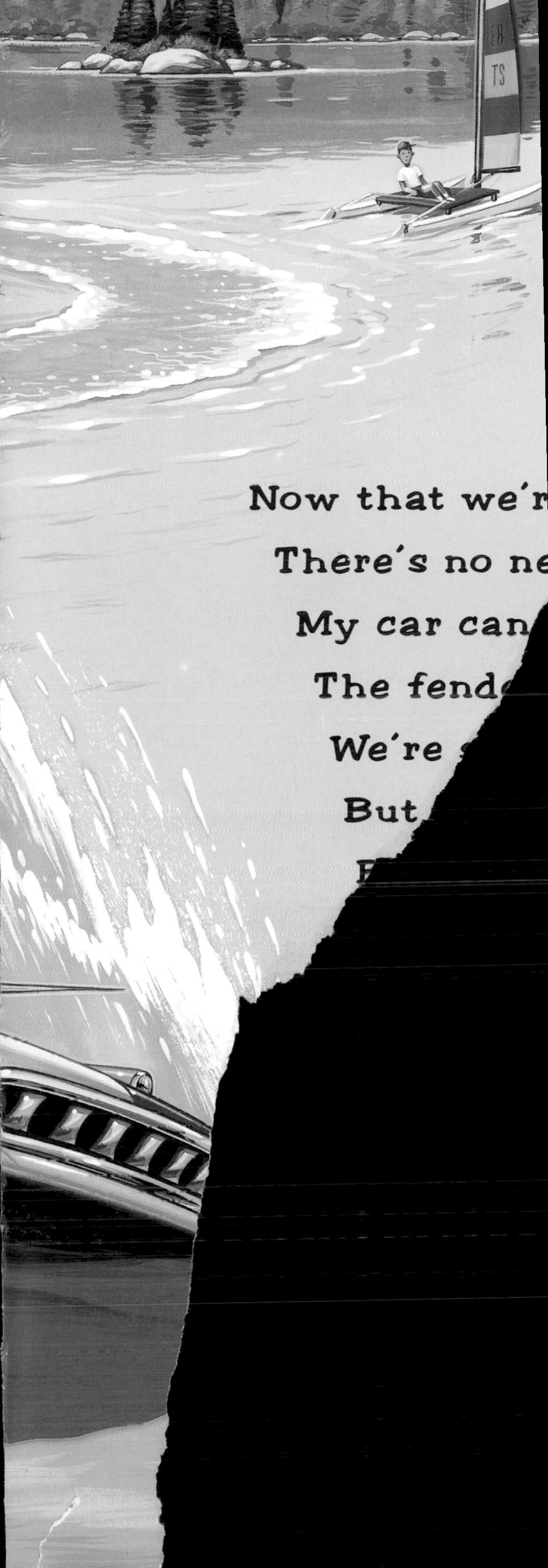

Now that we'r

There's no ne

My car can

The fende

We're

But

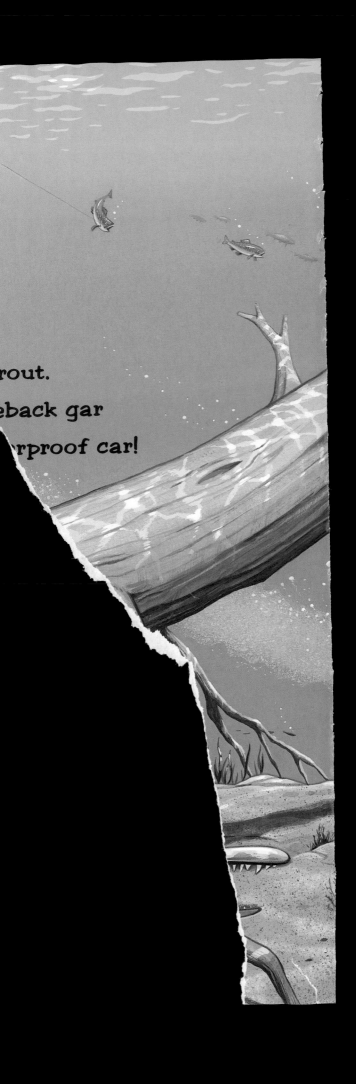

rout.

eback gar

rproof car!

Last but not least, the best feature of all

Comes down to a button that's shiny and small.

Push it and then, in the wink of an eye,

The car will take off! We'll be up in the sky!

We'll fly over land! We'll fly over seas!

To Alaska, Nebraska, Bermuda, Belize,

Or take a vacation when things start to freeze

And fly us all down to the Florida Keys.

My car will be cool! My car will be keen!

My car will be one big fantastic machine!

The toast of the town! The cream of the crop!

The belle of the ball and the tip of the top!

My car will be famous from here to Peru . . .

If I built a car, that's just what I'd do!

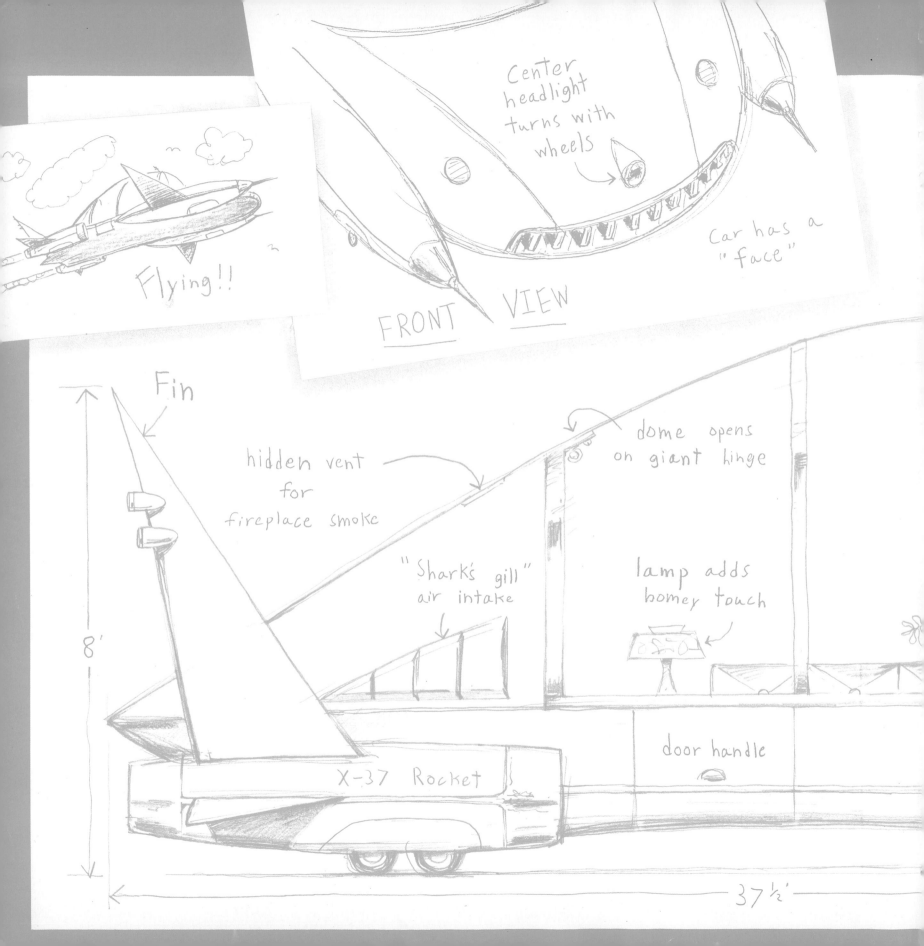

Flying!!

Center
headlight
turns with
wheels

Car has a
"face"

FRONT VIEW

Fin

hidden vent
for
fireplace smoke

dome opens
on giant hinge

"Shark's gill"
air intake

lamp adds
homey touch

8'

X-37 Rocket

door handle

37½'

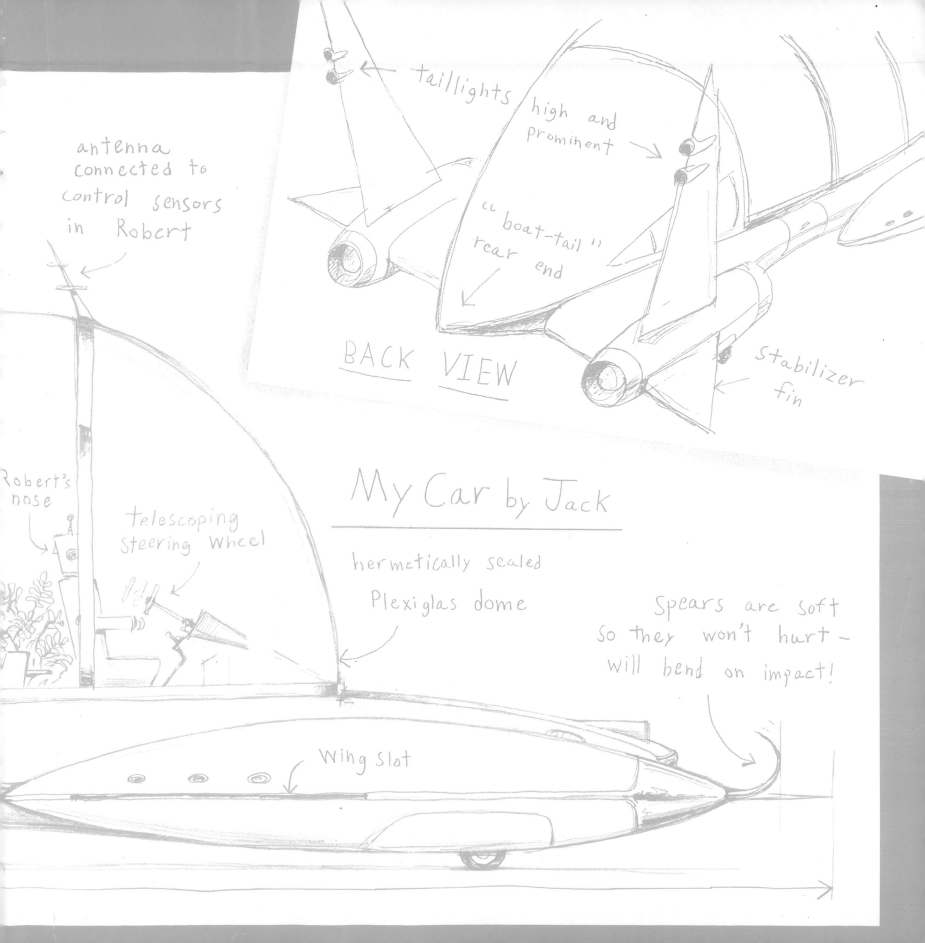

antenna
connected to
control sensors
in Robert

taillights

high and
prominent

"boat-tail"
rear end

BACK VIEW

Stabilizer
fin

Robert's
nose

telescoping
steering Wheel

My Car by Jack

hermetically sealed
Plexiglas dome

Spears are soft
so they won't hurt—
will bend on impact!

Wing Slot